WARRIORS

WARRIORS: THE NEW PROPHECY

WARRIORS MANGA

WARRIORS

CATS OF THE CLANS

ERIN HUNTER

HarperCollins*Publishers*

Cats of the Clans

Text copyright © 2008 by Working Partners Limited

Series created by Working Partners Limited

Illustrations copyright © 2008 by Wayne McLoughlin

All rights reserved. Printed in the United States of America.

No part of this book may be used or reproduced in any manner whatsoever

without written permission except in the case of brief quotations embodied

in critical articles and reviews. For information address

HarperCollins Children's Books,

a division of HarperCollins Publishers,

1350 Avenue of the Americas, New York, NY 10019.

www.harpercollinschildrens.com

Library of Congress Cataloging-in-Publication Data is available.

ISBN 978-0-06-145856-9 (trade bdg.)

Typography by Larissa Lawrynenko

2 3 4 5 6 7 8 9 10

First Edition

For India Holmes Coulson—welcome

Special thanks to Victoria Holmes

CONTENTS

THE FOREST

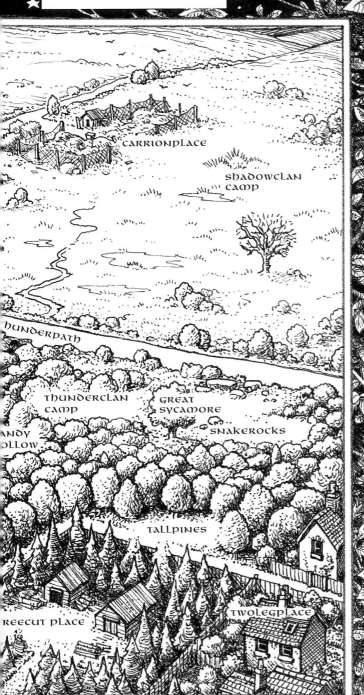

CARRIONPLACE

SHADOWCLAN CAMP

THUNDERPATH

THUNDERCLAN CAMP

GREAT SYCAMORE

SNAKEROCKS

SANDY HOLLOW

TALLPINES

TREECUT PLACE

TWOLEGPLACE

THUNDERCLAN

RIVERCLAN

SHADOWCLAN

WINDCLAN

STARCLAN

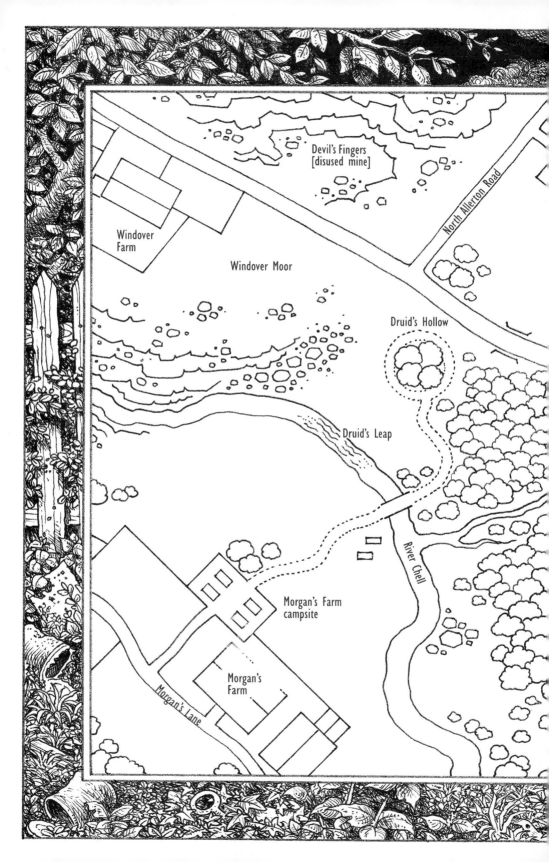

Devil's Fingers
[disused mine]

North Allerton Road

Windover
Farm

Windover Moor

Druid's Hollow

Druid's Leap

River Chell

Morgan's Farm
campsite

Morgan's Lane

Morgan's
Farm

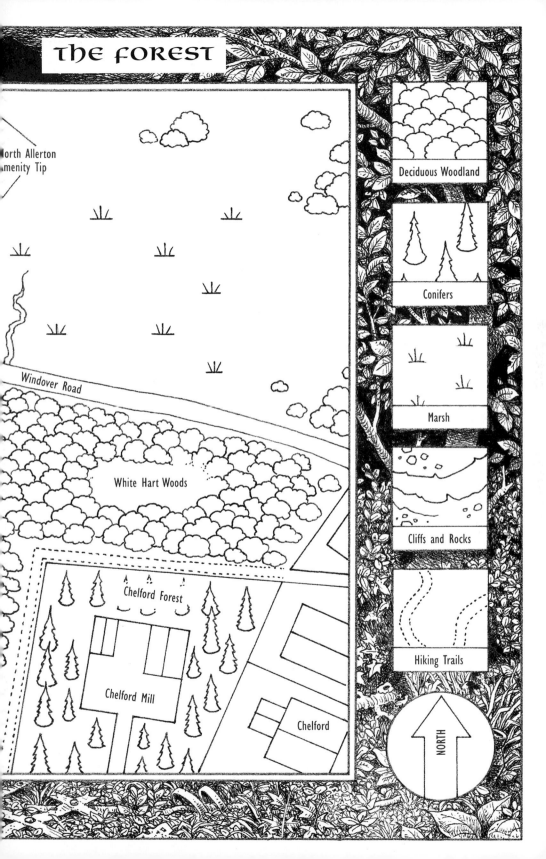

THE FOREST

North Allerton
Amenity Tip

Windover Road

White Hart Woods

Chelford Forest

Chelford Mill

Chelford

Deciduous Woodland

Conifers

Marsh

Cliffs and Rocks

Hiking Trails

NORTH

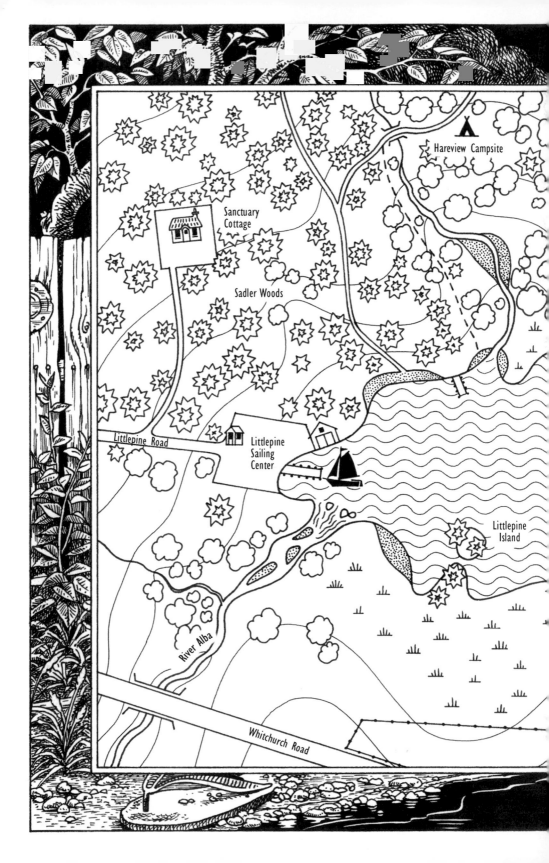

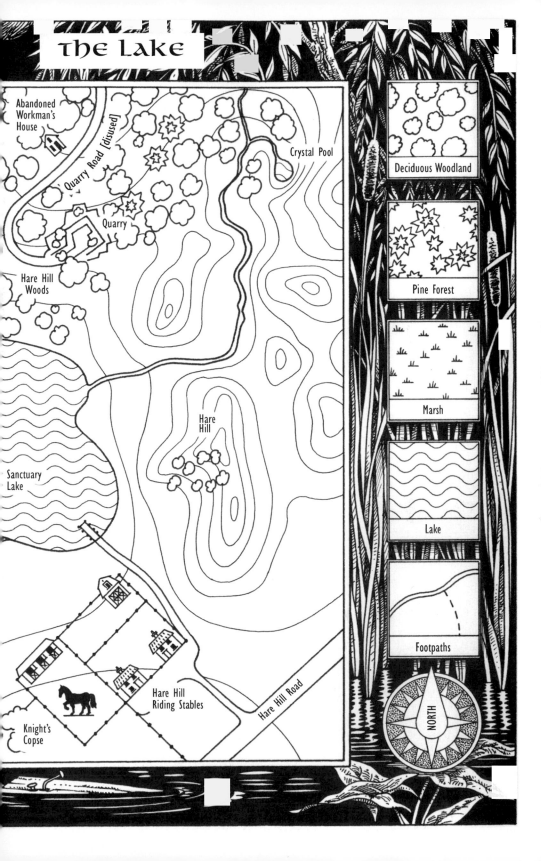

THE LAKE

Abandoned Workman's House

Quarry Road [disused]

Crystal Pool

Quarry

Hare Hill Woods

Sanctuary Lake

Hare Hill

Hare Hill Riding Stables

Knight's Copse

Hare Hill Road

Deciduous Woodland

Pine Forest

Marsh

Lake

Footpaths

NORTH

THREE LOST TRAVELERS

WHO'S THERE? Come forward, into the moonlight. Three kits, smelling of stars and the night? You're a long way from StarClan, little ones. Did you stray too far into the shadows at the edge of your territory? You must be surprised to end up here, far beneath the ground, with such a strange-looking cat to welcome you. I doubt my name, or this place, is spoken of in StarClan.

Hush, don't be scared. I won't hurt you. I'll show you the path home when day breaks, when there is light to see your way. Lie down—the floor is more comfortable than you may think. See how smooth it is underpaw? I would not exchange it for all the prickles and tickling things that line your nests. I have long forgotten how I ever slept amid such rustling. It is always silent here, apart from the echo of the water.

What did you say your name was? Mosskit? Of course, Bluefur's kit, Mistyfoot and Stonefur's little sister. And the underfed tom beside you? Adderkit, yes, from WindClan. You were very young to go to StarClan, weren't you? And named for the snake that . . . Yes, I know you too,

Blossomkit! Your white fur is unusual for a ShadowClan cat. Brokenstar may have promised you that you'd be a warrior before any other kit in the forest, but I don't think he ever imagined you going into battle. You died too young, but trust me, you were saved from even greater horrors.

Three little kits who didn't live long enough in the forest to learn about your Clanmates, their friends, and their rivals. There is a price to be paid in being a kit forever.

If you settle down—yes, even you, Mosskit—then I'll answer your questions about the cats you left behind. Ha, the night is not long enough to tell you everything I know! There are so many cats, many more than you know about. You would be here a moon and more to hear of them all. But I shall tell you about the ones I remember most clearly, and the ones I watch still. Oh, yes, I have watched them all, from as far back as any cat in the Clans can remember, and farther. And not only the four Clans that live beside the lake now. Much as they might wish to think they are the center of this world, there are cats of equal worth—or more—far beyond their fragile borders. Cats reviled for being loners and rogues, simply because they do not wish to live in a hive of chattering voices: poor beleaguered SkyClan, driven out because of their fellow Clans' selfishness; the Tribe of Rushing Water, who cling stubbornly to the mountains like the moss that grows beside the water-fall—I know them all. And BloodClan, who are not worthy of the name of Clan, and who will fade into the stuff of nursery tales once they have consumed themselves with their hunger for battle and bloodshed.

Who am I? I am Rock, the keeper of the world beneath the one your former Clanmates walk.

The watcher for more moons than you can dream of.

And the seer of all the moons to come.

Now, be still and listen.

THUNDERCLAN

I'LL BEGIN WITH YOUR mother's Clan, Mosskit. To many this is the noblest Clan, the Clan of heroes. But I take no sides; all Clans have their strengths and weaknesses, which differ according to whose story you listen to.

ThunderClan cats are impressive hunters; I'd even say I envied them their skills, but a life enclosed in rattling trees and wind-whispering leaves would not suit me. They have the skills to make themselves silent and invisible so they can hunt the little creatures that scuttle through fern and fallen leaf. You've heard of the hunter's crouch, when they gather their strength into their hindquarters before making the final leap? That is a ThunderClan trick; you'll not find it used by any other Clan.

ThunderClan has always been the fiercest guardian of the warrior code; if another Clan breaks it, you'd think every ThunderClan warrior bleeds from the wound. No cat could accuse them of being afraid to fight, as long as they believe the fight is truly justified—unlike others I could name, who seem to love the rip of fur beneath their claws and need no other excuse for battle. Hush, Blossomkit. Did I mention ShadowClan's name?

ThunderClan have had their fair share of border trouble. Back in the forest they quarreled with RiverClan over Sunningrocks almost every season. When the Clans first came to the forest, this little hill of stones was an island and belonged to RiverClan because they were the only cats that could reach it, by swimming. But when the river changed course the rocks were joined by dry land to ThunderClan's territory, and both Clans have laid claim to them ever since.

By the lake ThunderClan has faced a constant threat from ShadowClan on their shared border. For now Firestar has granted Blackstar's Clan hunting rights on the exposed stretch of grass where Twolegs come in greenleaf; a wise move, some cats say, because there is little prey to be found there. And another reason for ThunderClan to proclaim how fair and generous they are. I wonder how long ShadowClan will be satisfied with this addition to their territory?

FIRESTAR

Yes, Adderkit, I know the ThunderClan leader was born a kitty-pet, but it makes no difference to me where a kit gulps his first breath. Mind you, Firestar has given his Clanmates precious little chance to forget his kittypet roots. He is the champion of all cats who are not Clanborn. No cat could argue that Cloudtail is not a worthy warrior, or that Daisy does not serve the Clan well in the nursery. But you can see how other Clans are suspicious of Firestar's willingness to welcome loners and kittypets into the warriors' den.

What was your mother thinking of, Mosskit, when she brought this too-brave, too-curious kit into the forest? Was Bluestar blinded by the color of his pelt, knowing he fulfilled the prophecy that fire would save her Clan? StarClan wanted him as much as Bluestar did. Poor Firestar, he scarcely seems able to close his eyes without some farsighted dream filling his mind. But he has handled this burden well, lived up to all of StarClan's expectations. Maybe it took more than a Clanborn cat to discover Tigerstar's treachery, or to bring WindClan home after they were driven out by ShadowClan. See, Adderkit, you should be grateful to Firestar for helping your Clanmates. Blossomkit, they did not deserve to be chased out of their home!

Even Sandstorm came to forgive Firestar his kittypet roots—and she is a cat whose opinion is worth a moon of prey.

I wish Firestar nothing but peace, and a long life. Ha, empty words from me, who knows how every one of Firestar's nine lives will end.

FIRESTAR

BLUESTAR

YOUR MOTHER WAS a great leader, Mosskit, even if the price she paid for it was higher than she ever dreamed. She gave you up on that snowbound night, you and your littermates, so that she could become ThunderClan's deputy instead of Thistleclaw, who would have sliced through the forest until the paths ran red with blood. You should be proud of her for such loyalty to her Clan. Proud of your father, Oakheart, too, for raising your brother and sister to be strong, respected RiverClan warriors.

Was Firestar a replacement for the kits Bluestar never saw grow up? An interesting question, little one. She was an excellent mentor to the kittypet, and trained him to be a wise and confident warrior. She saw him as the savior of her Clan from the moment the sun struck his flame-colored pelt. Spottedleaf had told her that only fire could save the Clan, so Rusty must have seemed like a gift from StarClan.

It's too easy to say Bluestar went mad during the last moons of her life; you have only to think about what she gave up—including you, Mosskit—to understand how far she thought she had failed. Don't forget that she gave up her ninth life to save her Clan from the dogs, throwing herself into the gorge to lead them to their deaths. Stonefur and Mistyfoot found her on RiverClan's shore, so her final moments were spent making peace with her surviving children before she came to join you in StarClan.

BLUESTAR

GRAYSTRIPE
AND MILLIE

DOES GRAYSTRIPE HAVE any enemies, I wonder? Don't bristle, Blossomkit; not even ShadowClan is the foe of every living cat. He was the first to make friends with Firestar, when he was no more than a lost and curious kittypet. He and Firestar share the same foolish generosity: could you imagine any other pair of cats catching food for RiverClan when the river was poisoned, or traveling far from the forest to rescue WindClan?

But Graystripe's life isn't just a tale of friendship and heroics. Like Bluestar, he fell in love with a RiverClan cat, Silverstream, and he fathered her kits. It tore him apart to leave his Clan—and his best friend—when he took his motherless kits to their mother's Clan, but he believed it was the only place where they'd be truly welcomed. I think he was right; for all ThunderClan's noble gestures, they are not always kind to half-Clan cats. Graystripe came back when he realized that his loyalties were not to his kits' Clan, but to his own.

Now Graystripe has a new mate, Millie, a kittypet that he met when he was captured by Twolegs. I don't think ThunderClan realizes how much they owe Millie for the safe return of their leader's best friend and deputy. It was her determination that got them out of Twolegplace, her encouragement that helped Graystripe follow the Clans all the way from the forest to the lake. I hope he never forgets how much she has given up for him, and how far she has traveled from her home, in more ways than one.

GRAYSTRIPE and MILLIE

SANDSTORM

FIRESTAR'S LOYAL MATE, a good mother to Squirrelflight and Leafpool, she's the cat that won Firestar's heart after Spottedleaf died . . . Is this how Sandstorm will be remembered? She deserves more than that, in my opinion. If it weren't for her, Firestar might not have led his Clanmates into battle against BloodClan at all. I see your ears prick up, little kits. In spite of StarClan's prophecies and Firestar's determination to save the forest from Scourge, Sandstorm was the one who made Firestar believe he was doing the right thing by fighting the cats from Twolegplace. He trusted her because she loved him above all, and would never sacrifice his life for the good of the Clan. She knows Firestar better than he realizes—better even than Spottedleaf, for all the medicine cat's murmuring in Firestar's sleeping ears.

Sandstorm isn't just Firestar's shadow, either. Her courage matched his on the journey to rebuild SkyClan. She took on the role of medicine cat to help the scattered Clanmates, and she matched Firestar blow for blow in the battle against the rats, even though she had only a single life to lose.

I hold Sandstorm in higher esteem than I do almost any other Clan cat. She has traveled far from the days when she and Dustpaw tormented Rusty the kittypet. I hope Firestar appreciates her journey as much as she deserves.

SANDSTORM

YELLOWFANG

YOU KNOW YELLOWFANG, don't you? She walks among the stars now. Mosskit, if she's grumpy then it's your fault for disturbing her! She deserves more respect than you realize. And remember that she was once your Clanmate too, Blossomkit.

Yellowfang's troubled life took her from ShadowClan, where she was born and trained as a medicine cat, to ThunderClan, where she died in a fire, helping her adopted Clanmates escape. She was cranky, stubborn, impatient—and the most loyal cat you could ever meet. Her whole life was a quest for loyalty—first to ShadowClan, to her role as their medicine cat, to the son that she bore in secret. His father was Raggedstar, leader of ShadowClan. Foolish Yellowfang! She knew medicine cats aren't supposed to have mates, and especially not kits. When her kit Brokenstar became ShadowClan's leader and made the forest run with the blood of kits too young to fight, Yellowfang's loyalty to what she knew to be right sent her fleeing across the border to ThunderClan.

She blamed herself for Brokenstar's brutality, you know. Why else would she persuade Bluestar to let him live in the ThunderClan camp? I can't imagine what agony Yellowfang felt when she discovered he had plotted against the Clan that had given him food and shelter. Agony enough to kill her ungrateful son, I know that much. Brave, loyal Yellowfang, who fought enough battles for nine lifetimes.

YELLOWFANG

CINDERPELT

THE CAT WHO SHOULD have been a warrior, and the cat who was given a second chance. No, Mosskit, StarClan did not plan for Cinderpelt to be struck on the Thunderpath instead of Bluestar. Your warrior ancestors were as horrified as any of the forest cats when Cinderpelt ended up in Tigerstar's trap, and had her warrior path snatched from her.

She was a good medicine cat; there's no doubt of that. She should have been, given Yellowfang as her mentor. But StarClan did not whisper in her ear as clearly as they have done to other medicine cats. Remember the fire-and-tiger prophecy, the burning blades of grass that she interpreted as a warning that Brambleclaw and Squirrelflight would unite to destroy ThunderClan? She was wrong. Their quest to the sundrown-place saved the Clan by finding them a new home.

But StarClan did not blame Cinderpelt for that. She should never have been a medicine cat; they knew that right from the start. They gave her one more test before deciding to give her a second chance: they told her when she would die, and then let her live with that knowledge even though her apprentice, Leafpool, was on the brink of leaving the Clan to be with Crowfeather. Cinderpelt lived in the shadow of her own death with such courage, such dignity, resisting the temptation to beg Leafpool to stay, that she proved herself worthy of a second life, plunging back into the forest as one of Sorreltail's mewling kits.

I hope your ancestors watch over her more closely this time.

CINDERPELT

Leafpool

T HIS IS A CAT WHO WAS never destined to be anything but a medicine cat. I see your eyes shine, Blossomkit; is this the path you would have wished to follow? From the moment Leafpool and Squirrelflight were born, each always knew where the other was, and what they were feeling. StarClan fostered this link because they knew Squirrelflight would be journeying far, far from the forest—farther than any Clan cat had been before—and they needed a cat back home to be aware of what she was going through. For a while it seemed that, young as she was, Leafpool knew what lay around every corner and over every horizon. She knew the Clans had found their new homes when they reached the lake; she knew that Brambleclaw would make a strong and loyal deputy for ThunderClan. She even knew that blood would spill blood before the Clans were truly settled around the lake—and she watched with her own eyes as Brambleclaw killed his half brother, Hawkfrost, to save Firestar.

But the one thing Leafpool did not foresee was falling in love—and with a WindClan warrior, at that. Yes, Adderkit, I'm sure WindClan warriors are the best warriors of all, but Leafpool was a medicine cat! Everything about their relationship was wrong, according to your warrior code. How could their love lead to anything but misery and ill fortune? Even now it echoes among the Clans, coloring their future in ways not even Leafpool can see.

Leafpool

SQUIRRELFLIGHT

I F LEAFPOOL IS LIKE WATER, calm, deep running, reflecting the stars, then Squirrelflight is fire. She has energy to scorch every tree in the forest, and a tongue that could leave scars in beech bark. I would trust Squirrelflight with my life simply because she is incapable of doing anything but what she believes to be right. No, Blossomkit, this is not the same as always telling the truth. Even Squirrelflight has her secrets.

It was bold of StarClan to let Brambleclaw take her on the quest to the sun-drown-place—though I recall Squirrelflight gave him little choice and would have followed him regardless. But she proved herself a valuable companion many times over, and returned a better cat for it. If she had stayed in the forest I think she would always have been Leafpool's little sister, the feisty apprentice with a habit of leaping paws-first into trouble. The quest proved she had the courage of her father, Firestar, and the quiet determination of her mother, Sandstorm, which isn't always appreciated in ThunderClan.

Stormfur loved her first, you know. He saw something behind the mischief and the fire, when Brambleclaw saw only a quarrelsome nuisance. And Ashfur, though he would have been loyal to the end, failed to appreciate the strength beneath her impulsive ways. Squirrelflight needed someone to match her fire, not contain it, and that cat was always going to be Brambleclaw.

Squirrelflight and Brambleclaw have gone through so much together. Squirrelflight is a good mother to Jaypaw, Hollypaw, and Lionpaw. I hope Squirrelflight is well rewarded for her devotion.

SQUIRRELFLIGHT

BRAMBLECLAW

THE SON OF TIGERSTAR was always going to walk a path of light and shadow. He must feel sometimes as if his whole life has been spent trying to prove his loyalty to ThunderClan. He was the first cat chosen to go to the sun-drown-place, and if Bluestar didn't hesitate to trust him, maybe his Clanmates should follow her lead. I don't think even Firestar could have led the other cats on the quest to find Midnight; his curiosity, his generous spirit, would have distracted him, kept him helping those he met along the way. But Brambleclaw didn't stop until he reached the cliffs, until he heard what Midnight had to tell him. Then he came back to the forest and repeated the journey, this time with his Clan and the other three Clans, seeking a new and safer home. What further proof do you need that this is a noble cat, a brave and loyal cat who would stop at nothing to help his Clanmates?

And yet, and yet . . . he let his father, Tigerstar, walk in his dreams, mentor him in the pursuit of power; he even schemed with Hawkfrost, which showed extraordinary lack of foresight for an experienced warrior. Is his heart really as pure as he wants us to believe? Can Tigerstar's son ever truly step out of the shadows? You're looking at me round-eyed, all three of you, as if I know the answer.

I do, but now is not the time to share. Some things are best left to destiny to unfurl.

BRAMBLECLAW

ashfur

YOU'VE HEARD HIS name before, haven't you? Have the StarClan elders fretted over his destiny, about where his path will lead now that he has lost Squirrelflight's affection?

It's a shame Ashfur is most famous for quarreling with Brambleclaw over Squirrelflight. He really loved Squirrelflight, you know, even if he wasn't the best match for her. He tried too hard to protect her, to stop her from jumping in with all four paws when sometimes that's the only way Squirrelflight learns anything. But Ashfur is a strong, brave warrior, one I'd want on my side in a battle.

Any cat in ThunderClan would say that he has mentored Lionpaw well, shaped him into one of the best fighting cats this Clan has ever known. Some might accuse him of being confrontational, too quick to argue when he doesn't agree with a decision. But look at Dustpelt: he was never Firestar's best friend, yet he is a courageous, trustworthy warrior who has earned his leader's respect. Even though Ashfur and Brambleclaw were once rivals for Squirrelflight's affections, there's no reason Ashfur can't be a loyal ThunderClan warrior. Be careful. If you listen too much to Squirrelflight and Brambleclaw, it's easy to dismiss Ashfur as a troublemaker out for revenge. But the other cats should listen to what he has to say. He has a story of his own.

ASHFUR

BRIGHTHEART
AND
CLOUDTAIL

I HAVE SOMETHING in common with Brightheart: cats shy away when they first see my face, too. Perhaps I have not always looked like this—perhaps once I had fur as thick and soft as yours, and my eyes were clear and could see more than shadows and moonlight. But if that was so it was a long time ago, farther back than any of your ancestors can remember.

But Brightheart can remember what she looked like before Tigerstar's half-trained pack of dogs attacked her. It breaks her heart every time she sees her reflection—why do you think she never goes down to the lake? She is brave to her Clanmates, hardly flinches when a newcomer or a kit shrieks at the sight of her scars. But her first warrior name, Lostface, echoes in her ears whenever she is alone. If only she could see inside herself, to the beauty that lies in courage and loyalty and devotion.

Cloudtail alone has never flinched. But then, he knows what it means to be different, not just because of his fluffy white pelt. He is even more conspicuous than you, Blossomkit! Firestar's kittypet sister, Princess, gave her firstborn kit to be raised as a ThunderClan warrior, as if becoming a forest cat were as easy as putting on a Twoleg collar. Cloudtail struggled from the start—he even went back to the kittypet life until StarClan, and Firestar, gave him a second chance by rescuing him. Even now he doesn't believe in StarClan. But he does believe in loyalty and protecting his Clan, and the warrior code requires nothing more.

BRIGHTHEART

JAYPAW, HOLLYPAW,
AND
LIONPAW

THERE WILL BE THREE, *kin of your kin, who will hold the power of the stars in their paws.*

Firestar waited a long time for these kits to be born—waited in dread, not hope, because what would happen when kits were given a power even greater than StarClan's? Now they have come, and Firestar can do nothing but watch and wait to see where their paths lead—and whether his Clan will survive their destinies.

Lionpaw is the warrior, a hunter and fighter as brave as Tigerstar. But then, he should be, since Firestar's old enemy has walked beside him in the forest, training him and encouraging him to be ever more fearless. Would Lionpaw have been so strong and skillful without this cat of shadows?

Hollypaw is the thinker, the politician, sensitive and cunning and aware of all the different consequences that might come from a single action. For her, the warrior code is the root and reward of every choice a Clan cat has to make, and she would tread the hardest paths to defend it. Wit can be sharper than claws; remember that, little ones.

Jaypaw is the blind cat who sees in his dreams—and in the dreams of others, too. What else could he be but a medicine cat, with his memory for herbs and his instinct for StarClan's portents? But dreams are private, and I would hate to have my sleep disturbed by a trespasser.

Three young cats, with starlight in their eyes and the whisper of an ancient wind in their fur. Just remember this: power is neither good nor bad, but its user makes it so.

JAYPAW, HOLLYPAW, AND LIONPAW

SHADOWCLAN

AH, THOSE EVIL CATS! Their hearts have been chilled by the wind that blows from the mountains, and every kit is schooled to share his Clanmates' hunger for battle, for more territory, for the warmth of blood running beneath their paws.

All right, Blossomkit, put your claws away. I'm only repeating the tales told in nurseries of the other Clans. ShadowClan warriors are proud and fight well. Their territory is the least rich in prey—no rivers running with fish, burrows full of rabbits, or leafy trees hiding songbirds and squirrels. They share their territory with lizards and frogs, and the rats that feed on Twoleg waste in Carrionplace. Why wouldn't they seize every chance to add something else to their fresh-kill pile?

They are the night hunters, because ferns and brambles don't grow on their marshy ground. If there are no leaves and thorns to hide among, then darkness is their only cover for stalking prey. True, they use this skill to take their enemies by surprise as well, but does ThunderClan keep its hunting moves only for catching food? I think not.

No cat can deny that ShadowClan has been the cause of bloodshed more than any of the other Clans, in recent moons, at least. But the leader of the Clan is the cat who takes them into battle; you can't blame the warriors and apprentices for being loyal and running behind. They are trained to be fierce, proud, independent, ready to fight to defend their borders and their meager supply of food. If other Clans fear them, perhaps it is because ShadowClan are an enemy no cat would wish to have.

Sometimes it even seems that StarClan share the forest Clans' fears: they let Raggedstar die at the claws of his own son, Brokentail, and refused to grant Nightstar his nine lives because Brokenstar was still alive, albeit a blind prisoner in the ThunderClan camp. Maybe old scores are not forgotten, even by our warrior ancestors, and ShadowClan will have to battle for a long time yet against the better-favored Clans.

TIGERSTAR

IT WOULD BE INTERESTING to know whether Tigerstar counts himself a ShadowClan or ThunderClan cat; he lived far longer in the Clan where he was born; yet I've not known him to walk in the dreams of any ShadowClan cat, apart from his daughter, Tawnypelt, who wouldn't listen. But I won't be the cat to ask him; the shadowy forest where he walks now is not for me; nor should you try to find it, curious kits! This is far enough for you to wander.

I can hear your claws scratch the stone floor at the mention of Tigerstar's name. Is his bloodstained history used to scare mischievous kits even in StarClan? From the moment he saw an opportunity to kill Redtail, his own deputy, Tigerstar's path swelled the ranks of StarClan more than any other single warrior has done. Shall we list the memorable dead? Redtail, Runningwind, Brindleface, Swiftpaw and Bluestar, and Stonefur; and we can blame him for all the deaths in the battle with BloodClan, for it was he who brought Scourge to the forest. Foolish, proud Tigerstar, killed by his own ambition. He was the greatest warrior the forest has ever known, and the bravest in battle.

Now he walks a forest of shadows with his half-Clan son, Hawkfrost, for company. I wonder if Tigerstar remembers, when he looks at the cat beside him, his purge of half-Clan blood as leader of TigerClan. They still whisper in the ears of kits who show the same promise they once did—fierce fighters with ambition and pride.

Lionpaw should be careful. These cats are not his allies.

TIGERSTAR

BROKENSTAR

IT'S ALL RIGHT, BLOSSOMKIT; you're safe here. Brokenstar would not dare venture into these tunnels—for more reasons than a fear of the dark. For once the nursery queens are not exaggerating when they frighten kits with his stories. Even his birth was forbidden by the warrior code; StarClan's hearts must have sunk when Yellowfang, the ShadowClan medicine cat, fell in love with the Clan leader, Raggedstar. Yellowfang made her second mistake in giving her kit to Lizardstripe, a queen who made sure that the kit with the crooked tail knew he was unwelcome in her den. Brokenstar saw only one way of making his Clanmates respect him. He killed Raggedstar, not knowing he was sending his own father to StarClan, and set out to prove that he was the strongest, most fearless warrior in the history of the Clans.

Your warrior ancestors could only watch helplessly as Brokenstar led his Clan against WindClan, driving them out of their home; next they turned on ThunderClan, jealous of their prey-rich trees, and Spottedleaf died in their raids. Even after he was blinded and taken prisoner by ThunderClan, spared after Yellowfang pleaded for mercy, Brokenstar plotted with Darkstripe and Tigerstar to attack the Clan that had given him shelter. It is fitting that he did not die a warrior's death, struck down in battle, but was forced to eat deathberries by his own mother. Yellowfang avenged your death, Blossomkit, and all the deaths of kits forced to train as warriors too young.

BROKENSTAR

BLACKSTAR

SHADOWCLAN WILL HAVE TO go through many, many leaders to shake off the echoes of Brokenstar's and Tigerstar's deadly reigns: Nightstar, Brokenstar, and now Blackstar. Blackstar was Nightstar's deputy, and then Tigerstar's, and after Nightstar's timid, tortured leadership, Tigerstar must have seemed like the cat who would lead ShadowClan back to the days when they were feared and respected throughout the forest. No cat can envy Blackstar for having to follow in his paw steps, swimming with blood and with the Clan in tatters. He has done well to rally his Clanmates, to lead them on the Great Journey and build them a new home by the lake.

Blackstar never harks back to the days when ShadowClan won every battle, when it looked as if they really would take over the whole forest and make the other Clans serve them. He has made his Clanmates proud once more, confident that they deserve to be one of the four Clans around the lake, brave in battle and respectful of the other Clans at Gatherings. Mosskit, you can let your fur lie flat. If Blackstar has threatened the ThunderClan border, perhaps it is because, yet again, ShadowClan has been given the territory least rich in prey.

Blackstar has a long way to go before the other Clans forget ShadowClan's battle-hungry past. But he should not be punished for having pride in his Clan.

BLACKSTAR

TAWNYPELT

THUNDERCLAN CATS WOULD find it much easier to hate and fear ShadowClan if one of their trusted Clanmates had not chosen to make her home with them! Perhaps they should respect her judgment more; Tawnypelt was no supporter of Tigerstar, but she was punished for his crimes when she lived in ThunderClan by her Clanmates' lack of trust. Brambleclaw was willing to spend his whole life proving himself worthy to be part of ThunderClan; Tawnypelt preferred to find a place to live where she would be judged on her own terms.

StarClan chose Tawnypelt to represent ShadowClan on the journey to find Midnight, a choice that was perhaps meant to challenge ThunderClan, to show them that Tawnypelt had found her true home. The quest would have been less successful without her willingness to look beyond Clan boundaries. She recognized Crowfeather's strengths before her companions did, and Feathertail would have fought much harder not to fall in love with the WindClan warrior if Tawnypelt hadn't encouraged her.

Tawnypelt believes she can be a loyal ShadowClan cat without any darkness of heart or purpose. When Tigerstar summoned her to his shadowy forest in her dreams, she refused to listen to him. She knew he couldn't help her achieve what she wants most: loyalty and security and peace. She will go into battle for ShadowClan, yet she never forgets her kinship in ThunderClan, either. She has proved that being loyal does not have to mean treating others as your enemy. You should be proud of Tawnypelt, Blossomkit. She and her kits could do much to salvage ShadowClan's reputation.

TAWNYPELT

BOULDER

THE SHADOWCLAN CAT who was raised in BloodClan; the cat who led Tigerstar to Scourge and sealed the deadly pact that would bathe the forest in blood. The foolish, hapless warrior whose desire to impress Tigerstar made him forget the nature of his birth Clan, made him think Scourge would really be swayed by the promise of a few trees to hunt among. He's not an evil cat, and never tried to serve any dark ambitions of his own. He just had too much faith in the warrior code. Boulder lived as wretched a life in BloodClan as any other young cat. When he met a forest cat who told him about how the Clans lived, with warriors and apprentices and well-defended borders, Boulder left BloodClan and went to live among pine trees and learned how to chase frogs. His memories of living in Twolegplace faded to nightmares, then dreams, then half-remembered images of red stone and stinking alleys and furtive conversations. What he did remember was the possible advantage of bringing a fierce, bloodthirsty group of cats to fight on his Clan's behalf. Better to spill the blood of other cats than their own, especially cats who had made his early life a misery.

He paid a high price for his misjudgment.

BOULDER

LittleCloud
and
RunningNose

RUNNINGNOSE TRIED SO hard to save your life, Blossomkit. You were the third kit he'd seen that day with fur ripped away, your pelt stained scarlet like a deathberry. He'd been trained as a medicine cat by Yellowfang, but all his knowledge of herbs could not stop your tiny life from melting away like a snowflake on a rock.

Runningnose must have regretted the day he asked to become Yellowfang's apprentice. As Brokenstar's medicine cat, he was forced to interpret omens that promised nothing but success in battle for his bloodthirsty leader, and then tried to stop the lifeblood of the Clan from sinking into the ground as apprentices were taken from the nursery. Even after Brokenstar was captured by ThunderClan, Runningnose had more secrets to keep: this time, the fact that StarClan would not grant Nightstar his nine lives. His conscience must have weighed heavier than stone.

Littlecloud was Runningnose's apprentice. He was inspired to follow this path by the ThunderClan medicine cat, Cinderpelt. She rescued him during ShadowClan's Great Sickness, when disease from the rats at Carrionplace sliced through the warriors sharper than a badger's claw. Cinderpelt was punished for raiding ThunderClan's store of herbs to cure two ShadowClan apprentices, but ThunderClan has been rewarded by the presence of a fair and peaceful medicine cat in their rival Clan, who will never forget the debt he owes.

LITTLECLOUD AND RUNNINGNOSE

WINDCLAN

ARE YOU SITTING a little straighter, Adderkit? You should be proud of your birth Clan, whatever other cats might say about Brokenstar driving you from your home, or your Clanmates' willingness to make alliances to protect their borders. There is a great difference between being weak—which your Clan is not—and being vulnerable, which is the price paid for living on the moor. Your Clan has spent many moons learning how to survive in the open, where speed and a sense of danger count for more than stealth and stalking skills. And they are nearer to StarClan, up on their hill beneath the open sky; perhaps that explains why their warrior ancestors have spared them many times over.

    It's not always easy to befriend a WindClan cat—they have become like the rabbits they chase: suspicious and quickly startled, fiercely protective of their Clanmates. But they know that they are in less danger from allies than enemies, which is why they have a reputation for being a peaceful Clan, the least likely to invade another Clan's territory for food or power. Since Firestar came to the forest he has watched them join with RiverClan, then ThunderClan, and even fall under the thrall of ShadowClan when that seemed the only way to protect themselves against a worse attack. Whatever their enemies say, this farsightedness is a strength, and it is a mistake to think WindClan cats are ever truly loyal to any but their own Clan.

They suffered most when the Twolegs made the Thunderpath in the forest wider. They watched huge yellow monsters turn their territory to rabbitless mud, then became prey themselves as the Twolegs tried first to poison them, then rounded them up and imprisoned them. They showed great courage in not fleeing the forest long before the other Clans made up their minds to leave. For as long as there are cats living by the lake, WindClan will be among them, swift pawed and watchful, clinging to the warrior code like moss to a rock.

TALLSTAR

TALLSTAR KILLED THE snake that bit you; did you know that, Adderkit? He spent nine long lives fighting for his Clan, defending the borders, forging alliances that would grant his Clanmates one more moon of peace, and battling the creatures within his territory that wanted to harm his kits. Some cats thought he was too quick to make friends with other Clans, too willing to let another leader take responsibility for the safety of his Clanmates. But what was he supposed to do when Firestar and Graystripe risked their lives to bring his Clan home from the Thunderpath? Gratitude and respect for two brave young warriors is not the same as rolling over and showing the soft parts of your underbelly.

Tallstar fought as fiercely as a lion when he needed to, but he preferred not to watch his Clanmates bleed scarlet onto the grass. When Bluestar tried to lead her Clan into battle against him, believing his cats had stolen prey from ThunderClan territory, Tallstar trusted Firestar's warning that Bluestar was mistaken, and refused to fight.

He gave up his ninth life at the end of the Great Journey, knowing he had led his Clan safely to their new home. And with his last breath, all his wisdom, all his farsightedness, deserted him. Suspicious of his deputy Mudclaw's ambition, he made Onewhisker his deputy instead, thus cheating Mudclaw of becoming leader. Foolish Tallstar. He should have known that Mudclaw would harbor a grudge in his heart like a poisonous thorn. He must have watched in dismay as his final decision nearly destroyed the Clan he had struggled for so long to protect.

TALLSTAR

ONESTAR

T HIS CAT COULD TELL you a tale or two about the loneliness of power. He was a good friend to Firestar from the moment they met on the journey back from the Thunderpath; the two young warriors recognized in each other a sense of fairness and ambition to serve their Clan. It was partly thanks to Onewhisker that Tallstar agreed not to fight Bluestar over her accusations of theft; and WindClan cats were treated generously more than once when they crossed the border. Firestar believed he could depend on their friendship forever, and was only too pleased when Tallstar changed his deputy at the end of his ninth life.

But Onestar could not be the leader of his Clan as well as Firestar's loyal ally. Suddenly the friendship that had supported him from across the border seemed like a burden, a debt of gratitude. Onestar knew the other Clans called him Firestar's kittypet, ready to roll over and have his belly tickled when it suited the ThunderClan leader.

He needed respect from his own Clanmates, too, many of whom had supported Mudclaw's claim. The only way to do this was to make his Clan independent, confident they could face challenges without running to ThunderClan. There were no favors owed or expected, no tolerance of border crossing or friendly patrols. It was a hard lesson for Firestar, but harder for Onestar. He missed his ThunderClan friend, especially in the early days, when he struggled to convince himself he had any right to be WindClan's leader. At the time when he most needed an ally he had to walk alone, and watch a long friendship ebb away.

ONESTAR

MUDCLAW

MUDCLAW WAS WINDCLAN's most senior warrior, made deputy because even Tallstar recognized that his own peace-pursuing leadership needed the support of a warrior not afraid to show his claws. Tallstar's decision to replace Mudclaw with Onewhisker was a terrible betrayal of Mudclaw's loyalty. Would Mudclaw have made such a dreadful leader? Yes, he was ambitious—but his ambition was to become leader of his Clan, and no cat can doubt that he would have surrendered all his lives to defending his Clanmates and the Clan's borders.

He wasn't the only cat to think he'd been cheated. He had supporters in RiverClan and ShadowClan. And while Mudclaw sought to take back the leadership that he'd waited for for so long, another cat saw an opportunity to divide the Clans from within and seize power over all of them: Hawkfrost, goaded on by his father, who walked in his dreams.

Mudclaw had no idea what Hawkfrost was doing. As far as he was concerned it was a fair battle, and his quarrel was not so much with Onewhisker as it was with Tallstar, who had not honored the debt owed to a loyal deputy. The attack failed, and Mudclaw was killed by a falling tree. Was this StarClan making their loyalties known once more, making it clear they wanted Onewhisker to be the new WindClan leader? Or a lucky strike of lightning that got rid of a troublesome cat and formed a bridge to the Gathering place at the same time? Little kits, there are some questions even I cannot answer.

MUDCLAW

CROWFEATHER

WHAT MADE STARCLAN pick this inexperienced, reserved, defensive apprentice to travel to the sun-drown-place on WindClan's behalf? He was the only cat in the prophecy who was not a full warrior, and the only one without an old friend on the journey. Mosskit, you may well say he was grumpy and unhelpful, but he agreed to go, didn't he? Crowfeather never once tried to turn back, fought as bravely as the rest against hostile kittypets and hungry foxes, and faced Midnight side by side with his companions, knowing he had a right to hear her message too.

Feathertail saved him, in the other cats' eyes, because she saw past his shyness and his sharp tongue and found something to love. He loved her too, with a quiet fierceness that nearly split him in two when he watched her die in the cave behind the waterfall. He chose his own warrior name to honor her memory, you know.

When Crowfeather fell in love again, this time with Leafpool, the ThunderClan medicine cat, I wondered if StarClan had forgotten about him completely. Or perhaps they were punishing him for some misdeed he hasn't yet done? It was always bound to end in disaster. It wasn't only Leafpool's loyalty to her Clan that brought them back to the lake; Crowfeather was the one who said they had to return to save ThunderClan from the badger attack. He loved Leafpool too much to force her to abandon her medicine cat duties. By letting her go, did he lose any hope of happiness for himself?

CROWFEATHER

NIGHTCLOUD
AND
BREEZEPAW

IF NIGHTCLOUD WERE A gentle, loving cat like Leafpool, or feisty and warmhearted like Squirrelflight, it would be easier to feel sorry for her. After all, Crowfeather took her as his mate to prove that he was loyal to WindClan in spite of trying to run off with the ThunderClan medicine cat. But she's a difficult she-cat to like, with her short temper and her possessiveness over Crowfeather and her son, Breezepaw.

Don't hiss, Adderkit. I speak only the truth as I see it, and what some might call the love of a she-cat for her kits I call jealousy and arrogance. Nightcloud should trust her son to prove his own worth, without leaping in to defend him first. And maybe she should remember that of all Crowfeather's mates, she is the one StarClan have spared to live side by side with him.

Breezepaw shares his mother's arrogance, but perhaps we can forgive his readiness to draw blood in defense of his Clan. He has heard the whispers about his father, the doubts that Crowfeather is truly loyal to WindClan, and the rumor that he has a weakness beyond the borders. Breezepaw doesn't know this weakness has a name, but he will not let his Clanmates think the same about him. He is what Onestar needs most: a fierce, brave warrior loyal to WindClan and with complete faith they can win every battle. But Breezepaw needs to learn that a battle is unfair from the start if there are secrets waiting in the shadows, and if the cats around him have left a legacy of mistakes and ill judgment that has not reached its end.

NIGHTCLOUD and BREEZEPAW

ḣeatḣeʀpaw

HEATHERPAW WAS HERE once, little kits. Just like you she sat below this ledge, imagining places and cats far away. But for her it was only a game, and the cats were members of DarkClan, which she and Lionpaw conjured up when they played in the tunnels. To Lionpaw she seemed like the bravest, most devoted companion he could wish to meet this far under the ground; but what made Heatherpaw so determined to meet her ThunderClan friend in secret? Did she think the warrior code would not apply to her? She insisted they weren't doing any harm, but Tigerstar and Hawkfrost saw the danger in Lionpaw teaching a WindClan apprentice their best fighting moves. I don't think Heatherpaw was guilty of anything but selfishness; she stayed loyal to her Clan, although luckily she never had to face her friend on the other side of a battle.

You could argue that Heatherpaw showed great courage in entering the tunnels to look for the lost WindClan kits, but would they have found their way down if they hadn't followed her first? Seven lives were nearly lost that night, seven more scratches to go uncrossed on my recording branch. StarClan had no power to save them down here. The river spared them, that's all.

Don't worry, little ones. It's not raining tonight; the river won't rise. You'll be safe till morning comes.

heatherpaw

RIVERCLAN

YOU COULD SWIM THAT river if you tried, Mosskit. Are you drawn to the rushing black water? Can you guess how it would feel sliding over your fur? You are half RiverClan, remember, and those cats are born with a love of water not shared by any other Clan. This means that they alone can take prey from lakes and rivers, so they go sleek and well fed even in leaf-bare, when other Clans go hungry. They're not so willing to share prey, either; they were quick to accept Firestar and Graystripe's woodland fresh-kill when the fish in the river made them sick, but I can't imagine the favor being returned. Although they let ThunderClan shelter from the fire on their side of the river, so perhaps I am doing them an injustice. I just find their pride too close to smugness; they say their territory is safe because the other Clans fear and respect them, but surely it's a matter of the other Clans not knowing what to do with one end of a fish? Rabbits, voles, and birds can be found on the fresh-kill piles of the other Clans, but they don't hunt for prey in the lake even though they all have territory that runs down to the shore.

The price RiverClan paid for living by the river in the forest was the invasion of Twolegs every greenleaf. They lived in little dens made of flapping green pelts that were planted in the field next to the water, and they filled the river with bobbing boats that scared away the fish. Did you know that more RiverClan cats were stolen by Twolegs than from any other Clan? For no more sinister reason than to be kept as kittypets; Twoleg kits would see a RiverClan cat sunning itself on the shore and want that handsome, glossy-furred warrior to live in their own nest. What's that, little ones? You've never heard this before? I'm not surprised; RiverClan keep quiet about it, even now, because hardly any of the warriors came back.

CROOKEDSTAR

ROOKEDSTAR WAS THE leader of RiverClan when Firestar came
to the forest. When he was a kit RiverClan won back the rights to
Sunningrocks, and the cats used to swim across the river and
stretch out whenever the sky was clear, just to taunt their ThunderClan
rivals. Crookedstar and his littermates played too roughly on the rocks
one day and he fell and broke his jaw, giving him his warrior name. From
then on he had to fight more fiercely, catch more fish, and defend his
Clan more loyally to earn the respect of his Clanmates; a less than per-
fect cat is not welcome in RiverClan.

Crookedstar knew that a united Clan, even if it contained half-
Clan blood, would always be stronger than a Clan that quarreled within
itself. He knew who Mistyfoot and Stonefur's mother was from the
moment Oakheart came to him with a tale of finding two kits lost in the
snow. It was obvious from the color of their fur and the scent that clung
to them. Crookedstar also knew that raising Bluestar's kits would pro-
vide two more strong warriors for his Clan, and give the ThunderClan
leader a weakness when it came to launching an attack across the river.
So he chose to be publicly ignorant about where the kits came from.

He was less welcoming when Graystripe crossed the river with
Feathertail and Stormfur. Graystripe's mate, Silverstream, was
Crookedstar's daughter, and Crookedstar wanted to have his kin in his
own Clan. But there was no place in RiverClan for a warrior whose
heart lay on the other side of the river, and Crookedstar did nothing to
stop his Clanmates from making it clear they could never trust
Silverstream's former mate. It was this cunning, this confidence and
farsightedness in dealing with his own Clan, that made Crookedstar
one of the strongest leaders the Clans have ever seen.

CROOKEDSTAR

LEOPARDSTAR

LEOPARDSTAR WAS Crookedstar's deputy, and became leader when Crookedstar lost his ninth life. She shared his pride and his ambition for their Clan, but she lacked his wisdom and tried too hard to defend herself against the other Clans. She couldn't see Crookedstar's attitude to half-Clan blood as anything but a weakness, which turned her against Firestar and his Clan of kittypet warriors. When Tigerstar took over ShadowClan and offered a way of making the forest pure Clan, with no petty fighting over boundaries because all cats would belong to one supreme Clan, Leopardstar formed an alliance that would nearly lead to the destruction of every cat.

She realized her mistake when Tigerstar combined their Clans into TigerClan and made himself leader, then made half-Clan cats fight to the death. Whatever Leopardstar had hoped for, this was not it. But she was trapped by her pride and couldn't speak out against Tigerstar—not because she was scared for her own safety, but because she couldn't face losing the respect of her Clanmates by admitting she was wrong.

Leopardstar saved her Clanmates by agreeing to join LionClan on the eve of the battle with BloodClan; thanks to Firestar she ended up on the winning side. But she has never forgotten how close she came to destroying her Clan, and if she seems hostile and defensive when dealing with the other Clans, it's not because she doesn't trust them; it's because she no longer trusts her own judgment, and fears for the safety of her Clan if she makes another mistake.

LEOPARDSTAR

GRAYPOOL, MISTYFOOT, AND STONEFUR

YOUR LITTERMATES, MOSSKIT! You should be very proud of them; they grew into strong, loyal warriors who served their father's Clan well. Yes, you would have made a fine warrior, too. It is RiverClan's loss that they didn't get the chance to raise you with them. Oakheart gave his remaining kits to one of the oldest queens in RiverClan, Graypool. He knew she would recognize their scent, but he trusted her to keep quiet. Mistyfoot and Stonefur never questioned that Graypool was their mother; they had similar-colored fur, and she treated them the same as any of the Clan's kits, so why should they? It takes two to make a lie: one to tell it and the other to believe it.

All three of you inherited your father's strength and courage, and your mother's good sense and fighting skills. Leopardstar made Mistyfoot her deputy, and they mentored Stormfur and Feathertail. But when Bluestar revealed the truth about their birth, they became the thing Leopardstar hated most: half-Clan cats. When Tigerstar took control of RiverClan, Mistyfoot fled across the river to her mother's Clan, but Stonefur was captured and killed by Darkstripe and Blackfoot on Tigerstar's command. Mistyfoot returned to her Clan after the battle with BloodClan. She'll succeed Leopardstar one day, which means a half-Clan cat will become leader. But it would be a foolish ThunderClan cat who thought Mistyfoot had any loyalty except to the Clan that raised her and her brother.

GRAYPOOL, MISTYFOOT,
AND STONEFUR

SILVERSTREAM

ILVERSTREAM WAS Crookedstar's only daughter, and the strength of his leadership earned her the respect of her Clanmates before she had caught her first fish. She was as dismayed as any of them would have been when she fell in love with a ThunderClan cat. She saved Graystripe from drowning not because she had been struck by his good looks from across the river, but because RiverClan were not in the habit of letting dead cats pollute their source of prey. Silverstream did not want to be in love with a ThunderClan cat; when they met in secret, it felt as if she were walking on thorns, and fish stuck in her throat when she returned to her Clanmates at the fresh-kill pile. But loyalty and love are two very different things: all my life I've chosen loyalty, which has made my path much simpler. Love makes cats risk everything for the sake of a few stolen moments, ears pricked for the sound of an approaching patrol even when one cat is on his own territory, and should be among friends.

In the end Silverstream paid the highest price of all, bleeding out her life on Sunningrocks as she gave birth to Graystripe's kits. Silverstream would always be a RiverClan cat, like her father, while Graystripe was rooted in the forest as deeply as the oaks.

SILVERSTREAM

FEATHERTAIL

ORN ON THE EDGE OF ThunderClan but raised in RiverClan, Feathertail and her brother, Stormfur, were obvious targets when Tigerstar brought his obsession with pure Clan blood across the river. They were imprisoned in an old fox den with Feathertail's mentor, Stonefur, and were forced to watch him die in a savagely unfair fight with Darkstripe and Blackfoot. Firestar, Graystripe, and Ravenpaw rescued them and took them to ThunderClan, where they joined their Clanmate Mistyfoot; like her, they chose to go back to RiverClan when the battle with BloodClan was over. StarClan chose Feathertail to go on the quest to find Midnight. Stormfur went with her; these two cats had been through too much to let themselves be separated.

Feathertail was known as a gentle cat, but she had the courage of a full-grown warrior as well as loyalty to her Clan and a firsthand knowledge of what it felt like to be persecuted. Perhaps this is why the Tribe of Endless Hunting made her the subject of their prophecy: that a silver cat would save the Tribe of Rushing Water from the mountain lion that preyed on them. The prophecy came true, but it cost Feathertail her life, plunging from the roof of the cave with the shard of stone that killed Sharptooth. A short life, then, but one that deserves to be preserved in the Clans' memory for many moons to come.

FEATHERTAIL

STORMFUR

S TORMFUR CAME TOO close to losing his sister to Tigerstar's pure-blood madness; there was no way he would let her go on the journey to the sun-drown-place alone. So he ended up watching her die in a shadowy cave far from the forest, as part of a prophecy belonging to some other cats' warrior ancestors. You might think that would give him reason to hate the Tribe cats forever, but instead he found a new home in the mountains, with the help of a Tribe prey-hunter called Brook. It seems too easy, doesn't it? Swapping a sister for a mate, and adopting a completely different way of life with cats whose troubles had killed Feathertail?

But nothing is ever that simple. Stormfur was already suited to the mountain life because he had the ThunderClan talent for stalking and leaping after prey. More than that, he could not forgive his Clanmates for betraying him to Tigerstar, and although he would have fought in any battle for RiverClan, he was loyal to the warrior code more than to the cats who shared his den.

But he was born a Clan cat, far from the mountains, and his adopted Tribemates couldn't forget that. Only Brook was willing to trust him, but we've already seen what pitfalls love can bring. Forced out by the Tribe, they followed the Clans to the lake, but RiverClan was even less accepting of non-Clanborn cats, and only ThunderClan would take them in. It was only a matter of time before the mountains called them back.

STORMFUR

hawkfrost

THE SON OF TIGERSTAR and a lone she-cat called Sasha, Hawkfrost would never be looked upon favorably by StarClan. Sasha brought her kits to RiverClan because she was too weak to care for them herself, and although the life of a Clan cat didn't suit her, she hoped it would give her children a better chance of survival than if they were left in the wild. She came back for them when she learned that the Clans were being forced out of the forest by Twolegs, but by then Hawkfrost and his sister, Mothwing, were warriors, loyal to the code they shared with their Clanmates.

Even before he knew who his father was, Hawkfrost wanted to take Leopardstar's place. He trained harder than any other apprentice, practiced catching fish over and over, even though the skill didn't run in his blood as it did in his Clanmates', and was rewarded by being made deputy when Mistyfoot was captured by Twolegs. He was clever enough to know that being Leopardstar's favorite did not mean he was respected by his Clanmates. For that he needed something more . . . such as a sister who was the Clan's medicine cat. So he tore the wing off a moth to convince Mudfur that his littermate was the right choice for his apprentice.

Tigerstar must have jumped for joy when he saw that one of his sons shared his hunger. He began visiting Hawkfrost in his dreams, and encouraged him to support Mudclaw in the rebellion against Onestar. It was Tigerstar's idea that Hawkfrost should plot with a ThunderClan cat who was already an enemy of Brambleclaw's to lure Firestar into a trap. But Tigerstar underestimated Brambleclaw's loyalty to his Clan leader; as Leafpool predicted, blood spilled blood, and the lake turned red when Brambleclaw killed his half brother to save Firestar's life.

HAWKFROST

MOTHWING
AND
WILLOWPAW

YOU MUST KNOW Mothwing's secret already, little kits. I should imagine she is a constant puzzle to StarClan, a medicine cat who doesn't believe in them. Yet they have let her stay, because they can see that she has studied hard and has only the welfare of her Clanmates at heart.

Unfortunately for her, knowing which herbs treat a stomachache is not her only responsibility. Hawkfrost's threat to reveal her secret meant he was able to force her to make false prophecies, such as the tale about troublesome stones in the river that led to Stormfur and Brook being driven out. When she was unable to receive warnings from StarClan, she didn't know about the Twoleg poison on RiverClan territory that started killing her Clanmates, and her warrior ancestors couldn't tell her where to find catmint when greencough struck. Terrified that her lie might be destroying her Clan, Mothwing confided in Leafpool, who began speaking to Mudfur in dreams on her behalf.

StarClan found a better solution in Willowpaw, the RiverClan cat who showed an interest in becoming a medicine cat while she was still a kit. She became Mothwing's apprentice and was visited in her dreams by Feathertail and Leafpool for the StarClan part of her training. Willowpaw accepts Mothwing's lack of belief in their warrior ancestors because she respects her in every other way—and well she should. For once I believe StarClan has acted in every cat's best interests.

MOTHWING AND WILLOWPAW

GATS OUTSIDE THE GLANS

DOES IT SURPRISE YOU how many cats there are who don't live in Clans, little ones? The cats you and your Clanmates watch over often act as if there could be no other way to survive except by the warrior code, but how short their memories must be if they have already forgotten the Tribe of Rushing Water, or BloodClan, or the contented rogues and kittypets they have encountered.

For the Clan cats, the warrior code has served them well, provided them with food and shelter and well-defended territories, as well as neighbors to turn to in times of greatest need. But the forest is not littered with the bodies of loners and rogues who have starved to death or been killed like prey, and kittypets do not swarm from Twoleg nests like bees to join the fabled Clans. There's more than one way to skin a mouse—some start with the tail, some with the nose, though it's been so long since I saw one I think I'd keep it in one piece and eat it whole, fur and all.

What's that, Adderkit? You can't figure out the difference between loners and rogues? Let me think how best to explain. . . . Loners are cats who live on their own, not as kittypets, and don't trouble the Clans. Rogues also live on their own, but they cause problems. That's how the Clans make the distinction, anyway.

RAVENPAW
AND
BARLEY

RAVENPAW'S LUCK RAN out the day Bluestar chose Tigerstar to be his mentor. That warrior was never going to appreciate Ravenpaw's love of peace, or his sympathy for the different sides of an argument. Tigerstar saw his apprentice's reserve as nothing but fear, and ended up making Ravenpaw scared for his life. After Ravenpaw saw Tigerstar kill Redtail and lie about it to the rest of the Clan, he was in very real danger from the cat who was prepared to kill to get what he wanted. Firestar persuaded Ravenpaw to leave the forest and live on a Twoleg farm with Barley, a loner who had a good life in a cozy barn with as many mice as he could eat. Here Ravenpaw found peace, and the chance to learn about himself without a warrior breathing down his neck, ordering him to pounce, strike, catch, and hide. Ravenpaw would still fight to the death for his friends, and he's helped them many times with food and shelter, but he is happier not following the path of the warrior.

Ravenpaw's companion, Barley, also found sanctuary on the farm. Barley was born in BloodClan, where he broke Scourge's rules by living with one of his littermates, Violet. When his secret was discovered, he was forced to watch Violet being beaten up by two of Scourge's followers—who also happened to be Barley and Violet's other littermates. Violet survived and was taken in by a kittypet who promised his housefolk would care for her; Barley fled Twolegplace and came to the farm.

RAVENPAW AND BARLEY

PRINCESS
AND
SMUDGE

STOP FIDGETING, BLOSSOMKIT. Don't you think you should hear about kittypets, too? Are they less important than Clan cats just because they don't hunt their own prey and let Twolegs pet them? Having food and shelter doesn't take away an honest heart or courage or loyalty to their friends. Smudge was Firestar's nearest neighbor back when he was a kittypet named Rusty. He was a plump, lazy cat who told tales of the wild cats in the woods who ate bones, and he couldn't understand why Rusty would want to live among such dangerous creatures. But he never forgot their friendship and was brave enough to come looking for Firestar when he started dreaming of the SkyClan cats. Loyalty, courage, and respect: would you expect any more from a Clan cat?

Princess is Firestar's littermate who went to live with different housefolk. When she learned her brother was the leader of a Clan of forest cats, she gave him her firstborn kit, Cloudtail, believing he would have a nobler life as a warrior than as a kittypet. It was perhaps not the wisest decision—Cloudtail didn't take naturally to life in the Clan—but it showed a rare degree of trust and hopefulness. Princess was a good friend to Firestar when ThunderClan lived in the forest, and she still sits on the fence and stares into the trees, wondering where he is and if he is safe.

PRINCESS and SMUDGE

BROOK WHERE SMALL FISH SWIM AND TALON OF SWOOPING EAGLE

I T'S JUST AS WELL TRIBE cats have no allies; they'd take until the next full moon to introduce themselves at a Gathering. According to tradition, they are named for the first thing their mother sees when they are born, although to my mind that would lead to a lot of kits being called Roof of Cave or Wall of Cave or Floor of Cave.

Brook met the Clan cats on their journey back from the sundrown-place, when it seemed that Stormfur was the cat who had been sent by the Tribe of Endless Hunting to help them defeat Sharptooth. From the beginning Brook saw Stormfur as a special cat, one with enough courage and skill to fight the mountain lion that had killed the Tribe's best cave-guards.

Brook came to love Stormfur for real when she taught him how to hunt hawks and eagles, using mice as bait. She loved him for his readiness to try new skills, and for his refusal to treat her differently because she didn't come from a Clan. And she shared his grief when his sister died fulfilling the prophecy that a silver cat would kill Sharptooth.

Brook's brother, Talon, was less accepting of the visitors, but why not? Five cats had crashed over the waterfall like oversize raindrops, bigger and heavier than Tribe cats, with different ways of talking and different warrior ancestors. He came to accept Stormfur because Brook loved him, but it was less easy for cats who weren't her kin.

TALON of SWOOPING EAGLE

TELLER of
the POINTED STONES

R STONETELLER, AS HE IS known less arduously. The Tribe of Rushing Water doesn't have a leader, a deputy, and a medicine cat, like the Clans; instead, it has a Healer, one cat fulfilling all duties. The Healer is always called Stoneteller because that is part of their role: to go into the chamber filled with pointed stones at the back of the caves and interpret the messages in the fall of moonlight on the rocks and in the puddles on the floor. Herbal skills are less important than they are in the Clans, but that's because there are fewer herbs and berries to be harvested in the mountains. The Tribe cats have survived without these supplies this long because they had no enemies at their borders, ready to wound and scratch.

The Stoneteller encountered by the Clans on the Great Journey is a proud cat, keenly aware that his Tribe clings to life in the mountains by the merest cobweb. There is scant prey, and what they can catch can also catch them, especially eagles, which are always hungry for a kit. Leaf-bare is long and cold enough to freeze bone, and even the eagles keep to their nests. In the Tribe's territory, a missed paw step leads to crashing death many, many fox-lengths below; another reason why healing herbs are rarely needed. It's not hard to see why the mountain lion made Stoneteller desperate to find the silver cat who would save his Tribe—desperate enough to take Stormfur prisoner when he fell over the waterfall. Feathertail and the other cats came back to rescue him, and Feathertail killed Sharptooth. Stoneteller was not too proud to be grateful to this faraway cat who had given her life for the Tribe. He buried her above the waterfall, with the honor given to the noblest cave-guard or prey-hunter.

TELLER of the POINTED STONES

CLOUDSTAR
AND
SKYWATCHER

I NEVER THOUGHT SKYCLAN would be driven out of the forest when they asked the other four Clans for help. Unseen, I watched in disbelief as each Clan gave their reasons why they could not share their territory—mostly because SkyClan were not able to catch their prey. Could they not have been taught? If kittypets like Firestar can learn how to stalk mice and thrushes, surely forest-born cats can pick up those skills? But no, the four Clan leaders insisted they could do nothing to help, and SkyClan, the fifth Clan in the forest, was forced to leave.

Cloudstar was their leader at the time, and although he stayed with his Clan, leading them all the way to the gorge, where they scratched a new home out of the sandy cliffs, he lost everything when he left the forest: his home, the borders he had patrolled for so many moons, his faith in StarClan, and worst of all, his mate, Birdflight, and their kits. They promised they would wait for each other, but it was not until Firestar and Sandstorm rebuilt their scattered Clan, countless seasons later, that they were able to keep their promise.

Skywatcher was the last descendant of SkyClan living in the gorge when Firestar and Sandstorm arrived. His mother had told him tales of their ancestors who watched the full moon from the rock jutting out over the gorge, and who lived in different sandy dens according to their role in the Clans. The cats around him scorned him for being mad, but his madness became reality when SkyClan arose from the dust.

CLOUDSTAR and SKYWATCHER

Leafdapple, Echosong, and Sharpclaw

THESE ARE THE CATS who became the leader, medicine cat, and deputy of the newly rebuilt SkyClan. Leafdapple was a kittypet with the SkyClan talent for leaping into trees, a sign of her ancestry that made Firestar invite her to join the Clan. She was also wise enough to realize that cats without her bloodline would need to be welcomed to swell the ranks, and strong enough to win their respect.

Echosong was pure kittypet, with no hint of SkyClan in her long, fluffy coat and delicate paws. But she dreamed of Firestar and Sandstorm before they arrived, knew strange cats would one day need her help. SkyClan's warrior ancestors had all but faded away when there was no Clan left to remember them, but they had enough voice left to call to Echosong; this and her quick learning when it came to healing herbs made her the clear choice for medicine cat.

Sharpclaw used to be a rogue called Scratch, with the SkyClan ability to jump and the courage of a fully trained Clan warrior. He will make a strong leader one day, but he has much to learn from Leafdapple, who might spill less blood as she builds her Clan.

No, Mosskit, you wouldn't have seen the SkyClan warrior ancestors among StarClan. They stopped watching over the forest when their Clanmates were driven out, and they walk in different skies now. But they have made their peace with StarClan, and the lessons have been learned.

LEAFDAPPLE, ECHOSONG,
AND SHARPCLAW

SCOURGE and BONE

MAYBE I SHOULDN'T have saved these two for last; you're getting sleepy, little kits, and there's not long before dawn. I don't want to give you nightmares for what little rest you can have before it's time to go back to StarClan. But I'm sure you've heard of Scourge already, the self-appointed leader of BloodClan, which was only ever a rabble of stray cats roaming in Twolegplace. No warrior code for them, no honor or loyalty to anything except themselves and finding their next meal. Scourge united them in terror, and made the alternative to obeying him much worse with the help of sharp-clawed followers such as Bone.

Scourge's greatest strength was his lack of any sense of right or wrong; without a code to tell him when to stop, he saw no harm in carrying on until his hunger for power was satisfied. But this was also his greatest weakness, because without a belief in StarClan, he had just one life to lose. Firestar took that life from him in the battle with BloodClan after Scourge killed Firestar's greatest enemy, Tigerstar, and Firestar could only watch helplessly as the ShadowClan leader died, losing all nine lives one after another.

Bone died in the battle, too, killed by a swarm of apprentices after he took Whitestorm's life. You would have fought alongside them, all three of you, if you had known that wise and gentle ThunderClan warrior.

Now, settle down and go to sleep, little ones. I'll be here when you wake. I have enjoyed recalling old friends and past enemies. They all deserve to be remembered.

SCOURGE AND BONE

KEEP WATCH FOR

POWER OF THREE

WARRIORS

BOOK 4:

ECLIPSE

Jaypaw felt his mother's tongue lap his ear. "Are you okay, little one?" she asked gently.

He ducked away crossly. "Why shouldn't I be?"

"It's okay to be tired." Squirrelflight sat down. "It's been a hard journey."

"I'm fine," Jaypaw snapped. His mother's tail was twitching, scraping the gritty rock. He waited for her to make some comment about how much harder the journey must have been for him, being blind and all, and then add some mouse-brained comment about how well he had coped with the unfamiliar territory.

"All three of you have been quiet since the battle," she ventured.

She's worried about all *of us!* Jaypaw's anger melted. He wished he could put her mind at rest, but there was no way he could tell her the huge secret that was occupying their thoughts. "I guess we just want to get home," he offered.

"We all do." Squirrelflight rested her chin on top of Jaypaw's head, and he pressed against her, suddenly feeling like a kit again, grateful for her warmth.

"They're back!"

At Firestar's call, Squirrelflight jerked away.

Jaypaw lifted his nose and smelled Hollypaw and Lionpaw. He heard claws scrabbling over rock as Breezepaw arrived. The hunters had returned.

"Let's see what they've caught!" Tawnypelt hurried to greet the apprentices.

Jaypaw already knew what they'd caught. His belly rumbled as he padded after her, the mouth-watering smell of the squirrel, rabbit, and pigeon filling his nose. If only it wasn't going to be given to the Tribe.

Crowfeather, Firestar, and Brambleclaw were already clustered around the makeshift fresh-kill pile. Stormfur and Brook hung back as though embarrassed by the gift.

"This rabbit's so fat it'll feed all the to-bes," Squirrelflight mewed admiringly.

"Well caught, Breezepaw," Firestar purred.

Jaypaw waited for the WindClan apprentice's pelt to flash with pride, but instead he sensed anxiety claw at Breezepaw. *He's waiting for his father to praise him.*

"Nice pigeon," Crowfeather mewed to Lionpaw.

Breezepaw stiffened with anger.

"And look at the squirrel I caught!" Hollypaw chipped in. "Did you ever see such a juicy one?"

"Come and see!" Tawnypelt called to Stormfur and Brook.

The two warriors padded over.

"This will be very welcome," Stormfur meowed formally.

"The Tribe thanks you." Brook's mew was taut.

Jaypaw understood their unease. By accepting fresh-kill, they were openly admitting their weakness. Hunting was poor in the mountains now that two groups of cats were sharing the territory. And yet

Jaypaw could feel fierce pride pulsing from Stormfur. There was a core of strength within him, a resolve that Jaypaw had not sensed before, as though he were more rooted in the crags and ravines than he ever had been beside the lake. *He feels this is his destiny.* The Tribe were Stormfur's Clan now. *There's more than just the mountain breeze in his pelt.* He had been born RiverClan, and lived with ThunderClan, but it now seemed that he had found his true home.

Jaypaw shivered. The wind had been sharpened by a late afternoon chill.

A howl echoed from the slopes far above.

Brook bristled. "Wolves."

"We'll get this prey home safely," Stormfur reassured her. "The wolves are too clumsy to follow our mountain paths."

"But there's a lot of open territory before you reach them," Firestar urged. "You should go."

"We should all head home," Crowfeather advised. "The smell of this fresh-kill will be attracting all the prey-eaters around here."

Alarm flashed from every pelt as Jaypaw detected a strange tang on the breeze. It was the first wolf scent he'd smelled. It reminded him of the dogs around the Twoleg farm; but there was a rawness, a scent of blood and flesh, to it that the dogs did not carry. Thankfully, it was faint. "They're a long way off," he murmured.

"But they travel fast," Brook warned. The rabbit's fur brushed the ground as she picked it up.

"We're going to miss you," Squirrelflight meowed. Her voice was thick with sadness.

Brook laid the rabbit down again, a purr rising in her throat. Her pelt brushed Squirrelflight's. "Thank you for taking us in and showing us such kindness."

"ThunderClan is grateful for your loyalty and courage," Firestar meowed.

"We'll see you again, though, won't we?" Hollypaw mewed hopefully.

Jaypaw wondered if he would ever return to the mountains. Would he meet the Tribe of Endless Hunting again? He had followed Stoneteller into his dreams and been led by the Tribe-healer's ancestor to the hollow where ranks of starry cats encircled a shimmering pool. He shivered as he recalled their words: *You have come.* They had been expecting him and they had known about the prophecy!